Party Animals

**To Freya, Amy and Neil,
and party animals everywhere. — T.M.**

To my dad for my mum. — D.W.

First published in the UK in 2007 by
Alison Green Books
An imprint of Scholastic Children's Books
Euston House, 24 Eversholt Street, London NW1 1DB, UK
A division of Scholastic Ltd
London – New York – Toronto – Sydney – Auckland
Mexico City – New Delhi – Hong Kong

HB 10-digit ISBN: 0 439 95051 1
HB 13-digit ISBN: 978 0 439950 51 0
PB 10-digit ISBN: 0 439 95531 9
PB 13-digit ISBN: 978 0 439955 31 7

Text copyright © 2007 Tony Mitton
Illustrations copyright © 2007 David Wojtowycz
All rights reserved.

1 3 5 7 9 8 6 4 2

Printed in China.

Party Animals

Tony Mitton and David Wojtowycz

ALISON GREEN BOOKS

Today is Monkey's birthday and his party's tonight.
There are so many animals he's going to invite.
There's going to be dressing up,
dancing and **fun**
For birds and for beasts and . . .
everyone!

Listen to the message that the chimpanzees
Bang out on their **bongos**
on their knobbly knees.
"**Come to Monkey's party**
in the jungle tonight.
Wear something **shiny**
or **beautiful** or **bright**.

"**Dream** up a costume
and come well dressed.
There's going to be a show
with a **prize** for the best.
And come with a **tingle**
in your fingers and your feet —

"There's going to be
dancing to a
funky-monkey
beat!"

Hyena in the dust going
hee-
hee-
hee.

All of them thinking,
"I've got to be there!"
But each one wondering,
"What shall I wear?"

Lioness hunts through all her frocks.

Hippo has a rummage through her dressing-up box.

Crocodile snaps up something new.

Flamingo thinks pink looks good in blue.

Off the savannah and out of the swamp,
They all come along for a
boogie and a
stomp.

From up in the branches,
from under the ground,
They all want to **shimmy**
to the **jungle-beat sound.**

The animals enter.
They all look **great**.
The music starts pumping, and nobody's late.
Everyone's looking, with wide-open eyes,
To try and spot a **winner** for the
Best-Dressed Prize.

Will it be the lean and lovely **Lioness?**
Everyone gasps at her **glamorous dress.**

Or how about **Hippo,** with **tutu** and **wand,**
Giving us a twirl?
She's the **pick** of the pond.

Or **Panther** perhaps?
He's a real **cool cat**,
In his sharp, stripy suit
and his mean, green hat.

Or **Elephant**, looking so hunky and swell.
He's a **jumbo** in a **jumpsuit** and it fits so well!

Monkey starts judging.

But, hey! Who's this?

A snake slithers in with a scowl and a hissssss.

"What are you doing, dresssed up in those?
You mussst know . . . .

ANIMALS DON'T WEAR CLOTHESSSs!"

The party-noise turns
to a breathless hush.
The dressed-up animals
wriggle and blush.

Then Monkey calls back,
"Well, I'm telling YOU,
When humans aren't looking,
sometimes
WE DO!

"Don't throw a hissy fit. Snakes alive!

Come on and party. Join in and jive!"

Snake slinks off with a frown and a **hisssss**.
The party starts up as if nothing's amiss.

...slithery Snake!

He's covered in glitter from tail to nose.
And do you know what?
It looks better than clothes!
He shimmers and glimmers
and dazzles their eyes,
And Monkey says,
"Snake, I award YOU the prize!

I crown you
The Best-Dressed Guest of us all.
Now, on with the party.
Join in with our ball!"

Baboons bound in with a great **feast of fruit.**
Bright-feathered birds all **fanfare** and **toot.**
Snake sings **karaoke.**
Guess which song?

Yes! It's . . .
"Animals Boogie
All Night
Long!"